Series 606A

STORIES IN THIS BOOK

The Friend of the Children

The Friend of the Lonely Little Man

The Friend of the Family

The Friend of the Fishermen

JESUS THE FRIEND

retold for easy reading
by HILDA I. ROSTRON

illustrated by
CLIVE UPTTON

Ladybird Books Ltd
Loughborough

THE FRIEND OF
THE CHILDREN

Jesus was the friend of children. He smiled to see them playing games. They knew He was their very own friend. Everyone loved Him and wanted to be near Him.

When the children saw Jesus coming along the road, they stopped playing and ran fast to meet Him.

7214 0058 2

Jesus was the friend of mothers and fathers, too. He listened when they told Him about their children.

A father said:

"My little boy is ill. Please, will You make him well?"

Jesus was glad to make the boy well again.

He made many other children better, too. He loved them all.

One hot day Jesus had been very busy. He had helped many people.

The friends of Jesus saw how tired He was.

They were walking along the road.

"Jesus must rest," they said. So they found a quiet place by the side of the road.

He sat down to rest.

Wherever Jesus went, people followed Him.

"We must listen to Jesus," they said to each other.

"He is our friend. He will help us."

The mothers and fathers and children who were following Jesus saw He was sitting down.

"Let us take the children to Him," they said.

The friends who wanted Jesus to rest were very cross. They did not want anyone to bother Him.

"If only Jesus would lay His hands on our children and bless them," said the mothers.

But the friends of Jesus said:

"We must send them away."

Jesus heard them.

Jesus saw the fathers and mothers and children waiting. He smiled, held out His arms and said:

"Let the little children come to Me. Do not send them away."

At once the children ran to Jesus. Mothers carried their babies to Him.

And He took the children in His arms and blessed them.

THE FRIEND OF THE LONELY LITTLE MAN

Long ago there lived a lonely man. His name was Zacchaeus (say Zak-ay-us).

He was so short he had to stand on tiptoe to see over other people's shoulders.

He lived in a fine, big house and had lots of money.

But he had no friends.

No one else went for a walk with Zacchaeus. He was never asked to other people's houses.

He walked all by himself along the busy street. No one smiled and said "Good-day!"

People had to pay him too much money for taxes. Zacchaeus was greedy, so no one wanted to be friends with a money collector.

One day Zacchaeus heard two people talking.

"Jesus is the friend of *everyone*," said one man.

"Yes, He even has a money collector as a friend," said the other man. He shook his head.

"I wish I could see Jesus," said lonely Zacchaeus to himself. "He must be very kind."

Zacchaeus listened and heard shouting in the street.

A crowd of people were waving and calling to each other.

"Jesus is coming. Jesus is coming."

The little man ran and stood on tiptoe; but he could not see anything.

"I want to see Jesus. Whatever shall I do?" thought Zacchaeus.

Zaccheus ran along the street to a tree.

"I will climb up and see Jesus," said Zaccheus to himself.

He peeped through the thick leaves to see Jesus passing by.

But Jesus stopped beneath the tree. He looked up and said:

"Zaccheus, hurry and come down. I want to stay in your house to-day."

Zaccheus was so excited. He scrambled down and stood by Jesus.

Jesus went home with Zaccheus. No one knew why He stayed with the money collector.

But Jesus talked with him. Then Zaccheus gave back a lot of money to the people. He felt much happier.

Zaccheus was not lonely any more.

THE FRIEND OF
THE FAMILY

Near the seaside lived a happy family. Jesus was their best friend.

There was Peter and his wife, and Andrew his brother. The mother of Peter's wife also lived in the house. Let us call her Grandmother.

Jesus liked to visit the home of this happy family.

Grandmother liked to be busy. She helped to get the dinner ready. She helped to cook and make things nice for the family.

Everyone loved her. She was so happy and glad to talk to them. Friends who lived down the street used to ask:

"How is Grandmother to-day?"

One day Jesus was in church. Peter and Andrew were there. All the people sang songs of praise to God, and everyone listened to Jesus.

They knew Jesus had helped many of the people in the church.

After the service Jesus went out with His friends, Peter and Andrew.

Jesus and Peter and Andrew walked home. Jesus was going to have dinner with Peter's family.

Perhaps friends who had been to church asked Peter how Grandmother was.

They all knew she would be so glad to have everything nice for their visitor, Jesus, the friend of the family.

When they came to Peter's house, all was quiet. There was no dinner ready.

Grandmother was so ill and so hot. They asked Jesus to help her.

Jesus took hold of her hot hands. Grandmother opened her eyes and smiled.

She was better as soon as Jesus touched her.

She got up and helped the others.

THE FRIEND OF
THE FISHERMEN

Jesus had gone away for a time. His friends were sad.

The names of three of these friends were Peter, James and John. They were fishermen.

Peter, James and John had helped Jesus before He went away.

They sat on a hillside and wished Jesus was with them.

Jesus had promised He would come back to His friends. So they waited for Him.

There was a big, blue lake at the foot of the hill, and they walked down to the shore.

Peter, James and John saw fishing boats sailing by. Children were paddling and playing by the edge of the water.

Peter, James and John grew tired of waiting.

The children had gone home. It was getting late, and still Jesus did not come.

Peter could not wait any longer.

His own fishing boat was not far away. He was able to bring it to the shore where they had been waiting.

"I'm going fishing," he said.

"We will come, too," said the others.

So they climbed down into the boat.

The friends of Jesus looked sad as they got the fishing boat ready.

They pushed it away from the shore, pulled open the sail and slowly sailed away.

All night the fishermen friends fished, but caught nothing. Not even one fish. So they sailed home again.

As they got near the shore someone called:

"Friends, have you any fish?"

They said, "Not one."

"Throw your net on the right side of the boat and you will find some," said the voice.

So they did.

When they tried to pull in the net, they found it full of fish.

Then John said, "It is Jesus!" He had come back.

Peter was in such a hurry to see Jesus that he jumped out of the boat. He waded through the water to meet his friend.

The fishermen dragged the net full of fish towards the shore.

There was a fire and fish were cooking, and bread was ready on the shore.

"Bring some of the fish you have caught," said Jesus.

Then Peter went and helped the others with the net. He brought more fish to be cooked.

"Come and eat," said Jesus.

So they all had breakfast on the shore with Friend Jesus.

Series 606A